W9-BWD-618

3 4050 0000 8333 2

WHEN TINY WAS TINY

by
Cari Meister

illustrated by
Rich Davis

PUFFIN BOOKS

PUFFIN BOOKS
Published by the Penguin Group
Penguin Putnam Books for Young Readers,
345 Hudson Street, New York, New York 10014, U.S.A.
Penguin Books Ltd, 80 Strand, London WC2R ORL, England
Penguin Books Australia Ltd, Ringwood, Victoria, Australia
Penguin Books Canada Ltd, 10 Alcorn Avenue, Toronto, Ontario, Canada M4V 3B2
Penguin Books (N.Z.) Ltd, 182-190 Wairau Road, Auckland 10, New Zealand
Penguin Books Ltd, Registered Offices: Harmondsworth, Middlesex, England

First published in the United States of America by Viking and Puffin Books,
divisions of Penguin Putnam Books for Young Readers, 1999

5 7 9 10 8 6

LIBRARY OF CONGRESS CATALOGING-IN-PUBLICATION DATA
Meister, Cari.
When Tiny was tiny / by Cari Meister : illustrated by Rich Davis.   p.   cm.
Summary: A dog's owner describes how Tiny grew from a very small puppy to a very big dog.
ISBN 0-670-88058-2 (hc.) — ISBN 0-14-130419-7 (pbk.)
[I. Dogs—Fiction] I. Davis, Rich, date– ill. II. Title.
PZ7.M515916Wh 1999   [E]—dc21   98-47827   CIP   AC

Puffin® and Easy-to-Read® are registered trademarks of Penguin Putnam Inc.

Printed in Hong Kong

Reading level 1.7

This is Tiny.

This is Tiny when he was tiny.

He fit in my shoe.

He fit in my bag.

He fit in my pocket.

Tiny did not stay tiny.

Tiny grew.

Now Tiny is not tiny.

Now Tiny is very big!

When Tiny was tiny, he dug in the dirt.

He still does.

When Tiny was tiny,
he licked me.

He still does. Yuck!

When Tiny was tiny, he had big feet.

He still does. Ow!
Get off my foot, Tiny.

Some days Tiny thinks he is
still tiny.

I try to teach him.
I tell him he is not tiny.

I tell him he is big.
I tell him big is good.

When Tiny was tiny, he could
not run fast.

Now he can. Wait for me, Tiny!

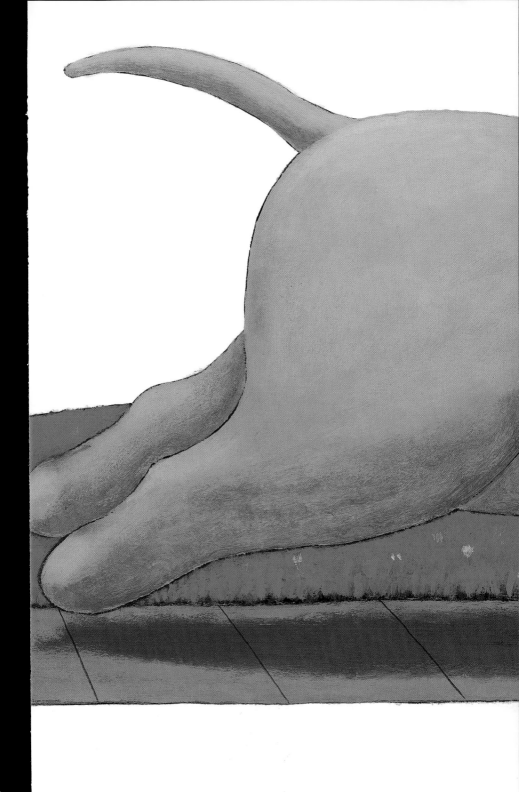

When Tiny was tiny, he could
not do tricks.

Now he can. Good dog, Tiny!

When Tiny was tiny, he was my best friend.

He still is.